The House Upon The Green Hill

A thrilling crime fiction and suspense novel

By Denise Graham

Table of Contents

Chapter 1

The lush greenness of the Virginia landscape was juxtaposed with the antique, orange brick house that rested in one of its hills. Crawling down its wall, the ivy bushes thrived upon it for one hundred years. As far as the locals were concerned, another bush of ivy would always grow through the decaying ones. While the windows and doors had been updated when Laura and her former husband purchased the house twenty years ago, the garage door still looked like it was close to crumbling.

Dominic drove his Chevrolet through the gravelly road while Laura and her two kids, Thomas and Ashley sat patiently. Dominic thrusted his way in as soon as the garage door creaked upward.

Was this built fifty years ago? It's falling apart like the rest of this damn house, Thomas thought.

Thomas glanced at Ashley who looked out the window at the dilapidating rags with her green eyes. She held the soccer ball on her lap. Her soccer uniform was quite tattered after practice. While Thomas

only wore his regular jeans and Van Halen

shirt. He brushed his short brown hair and

shuffled on his seat as he continued to wait.

Dominic let the car rest within, with

the old records leering down upon it and the

particles flickering around the single light

bulb. The trashcan nearby was overfilled

with oil-stained paper towels, which nearly

fell out at the top.

As soon as he turned off the ignition,

Dominic swung open the door and closed it,

which was enough noise to signal to their

dog Travis in the nearby yard that they

arrived home. Thomas glanced at Dominic who brushed his hands against his plaid shirt, wiping off any dust that met him. Marching out of the garage, he looked toward the house, where his new family would wait for him.

Ashley asked Laura, "Is Dominic alright with your trip?"

"I have no other options," she told her. "It's important for our firm if we can negotiate with foreign investors."

Thomas changed the subject by asking Laura, "Will I get the right information from the bank?"

"I'm sure you will," she told him. "I know Mr. Masterson. He will help you with any letters of recommendations."

Thomas anticipated enrolling in university as an Accounting major. He met Mr. Masterson, although he never had the opportunity to even open a bank account. Thomas remembered that day when met Mr. Masterson at the bank in the city of Columbia. It all happened before COVID-19 forced the bank to only allow a few customers at a time. Laura drove Thomas and Ashley, passing through the roads which weren't as crowded as it usually was during the afternoon. While cars and trucks were parked on the side in Columbia, the buildings looked practically empty even though there were people inside cajoling and laughing. It looked as though the people were enjoying their lives before the pandemic.

I always love the organization of money. And just how much it affects everybody in a positive way.

He said, "Perhaps I could write in my admissions essay about how I love accounting because it makes a functioning democracy."

"Sounds deep."

Of course, I don't think that Dominic would want me either way. Screw that old man anyway.

Then, Laura's phone vibrated. As soon as she got out of the car, she picked up the phone and talked to one of her executives.

"Of course," Ashley teased Thomas. "You'd have to worry about meeting the wrong girl who would just use your money skills for herself."

"Well," Thomas turned to Ashley. "You should worry about becoming a—" He waved his finger up and down at her soccer uniform. "…Literal soccer mom."

"Oh, screw you, Thomas. At least I would be fit whereas you'd just gain weight sitting all day."

Thomas knew Ashley had been interested in soccer ever since elementary school and had been practicing non-stop in Williams' large background where their black Labrador Retriever Travis would often join in. The conflict between Thomas and Ashley wasn't uncommon in the Williams' household, while it drove Laura insane, it merely entertained their stepfather Dominic.

Then, Thomas swiped the soccer ball from Ashley's lap as she leered at him and folded her arms.

She looked irritated as she reached out unenthusiastically to grab the soccer ball from his hands, but he kept bringing it away from her.

"What?!" Laura shouted. That loud question caused Thomas and Ashley to look attentively at her, as though they were being a nuisance to her driving.

"How are we going to get through this, then?"

She opened the car and continued to talk roughly toward one of her executives. Instead of asking what was wrong, the two teens simply sat still.

Thomas gave the soccer ball back to Ashley and then got out of the car. Upon arriving on the front yard, he observed the ivy bush as he always did, noting how the petals of the ivy had just started turning green, as though informing him that Spring was about to bring a new life.

Hopefully, it's a new life where I'm free from that jackass Dominic. Why can't he go back to his old family?

Within the bush, there were twiggy roots that abound, as though they were evidence of his attempts to pull it out, with Laura quickly stopping him and explaining to him that the ivy bush was important to the Williams family. It grew there ever since, as the legend goes, when an immigrant branch of Laura Williams' family arrived from England. It was said that there was an ivy seed embedded within the coat of the patriarch of the family who put his hand upon the wall. Some people in Maury County claimed that he was in a fight over a money dispute and ended up crashing onto the wall. Others claimed that his wife put up his coat to dry when a strong gust of wind carried the ivy seed into the wall.

Whatever the case, Thomas ignored it and walked inside the house where the only objects to greet him were the grandfather clock which *thunked* mockingly as usual and the turned-off television. He sat down at the kitchen in one of the chairs and watched Dominic petting Travis, as though he was like a child to him. He often told Laura about how his first marriage involved just one son while his new marriage included three children—Thomas, Ashley, and

Travis. Even though Thomas had yet to accept his new stepfather. However, Dominic spent more time petting Travis that he didn't know his new family just came home.

As soon as Ashley and Laura walked inside, Dominic told them, "I got laid off because the company couldn't afford to keep me."

Thomas was shocked and almost fell out of his chair, at the prospect that they would lose this house they lived in for generations. *Generations before Dominic at least.*

Laura approached him and asked, "What do we plan to do now?"

"I have no idea, Laura. Nobody anywhere prepared for this pandemic."

Laura turned to her two children and told them, "Go to your rooms. You don't need to hear this."

As soon as they walked through the hallways, Thomas went inside his room, which had posters of Green Day plastered all over the walls. He laid upon his bed with his hands clasped behind his head upon his pillow. He stared at the blank television in the middle of the wall, not bothering to reach for his remote control.

Will I ever pursue my dream as an accountant?

Instead of wanting to ask that, he instead got out of his bed and put his ear upon his door, so he could listen to the argument.

Laura asked Dominic, "Have you started looking elsewhere?"

"I don't know if they are also affected. We cannot move out because we don't know if anywhere else is open for sale."

Dominic put his hands upon his face, "I'm trained as an electrical engineer. That is my only trade."

"You know that it's valuable. I will help you find another job for that trade."

"Where, Laura?! You work for a real estate firm, so how would you know what goes into being an electrical engineer?"

"Nothing, but everybody uses electricity, so maybe you would find employment anywhere."

Maybe I can help?

Thomas opened his door and announced, "Maybe the firm could use an electrical engineer?"

Then Laura turned to Thomas and declared, "You don't need to hear this, Thomas!"

Thomas swung open the door and marched out. He said, "I do. We could lose the house if we don't do something about it."

"I'm not interested in what you want, Thomas," Dominic told him.

"We're trying to help you, old man!"

Although tension did exist between Thomas and Dominic, Laura looked shocked that he would directly call Dominic an *old man*.

"I look young enough to be your brother, boy," Dominic sneered. "A lot more than your other father."

Thomas never heard Dominic mock his biological father before and took a step away.

"Don't talk to my son like that," Laura warned him. "And don't bring John into this discussion."

Instead of exacerbating the drama, Thomas walked back into his room. As soon as he closed the door, he heard his mother shout at Dominic, "I didn't marry you so you could screw us over!"

Thomas didn't want to hear of any more arguing, so he brought himself to his bed, already exhausted from a day in high school. At that point, Thomas slowly went to sleep.

Chapter 2

As soon as Thomas awakened, he finished his homework. It was easier to do since there were no arguments around to distract him. He tried to enjoy the algebra, though he was hesitant to continue doing it. Instead he put his head back onto his pillow and stared at the wall.

Will I have to forego all of this? Do I have to spend time relocating just like after our separation from my real dad?

Then, Laura walked into Thomas's room and told him, "I know this is difficult.

The pandemic is affecting everyone.
Dominic may not be friendly toward you,
but we need to work together."

He clearly doesn't.

Instead of saying that thought,
Thomas simply said, "Are you still going on
this trip in the middle of all of this?"

"My job demands it of me. Otherwise,
they would find someone else, and I end up
demoted."

"Will I have to encounter *that* when I
become an accountant?"

Laura placed her hand upon his
shoulder and told him, "You are only

sixteen. Worry about doing your homework."

"I just hope that I'm able to go to college."

"You will. Mr. Masterson and I will assure you of it."

Mr. Masterson was quite a hospitable man, offering some of the candy at the counter for Laura and Thomas. He was quite happy that Thomas decided to pursue this career path, particularly since he would be able to make a lot of money.

"What do you want me to do while you are aware of your business trip?"

"Just take care of everything in the house and not drive your sister crazy."

Or Dominic, which will be hard.

She continued, "Dominic will most definitely have as much of the house sorted out, since he will need help with finding employment."

Then, Thomas looked to his math homework and dismayed hit him.

"I don't know if I would ever handle a pandemic like this."

"Nobody ever did neither. But now we know how to deal with it in case another one comes around."

Of course, Thomas felt that the germs were not the only parts that would seep behind the icy-grown walls.

The family met in the living room for one last time to prepare for Laura's trip. Dominic was the one who planned to drive through an uncertain road, and he hoped there was barely any traffic that he had to pass through. Laura was dressed in her pantsuit attire with her suitcase full of her important information.

It had been three days since the argument, though it appeared to Thomas that

Dominic had forgotten it—or at least had bottled it.

"I'm getting tired," Dominic told Laura. "Of being told that I have white male privilege by the fake news media. It didn't protect me from losing my job."

Politically, there was no difference between Dominic and Laura. However, Dominic was more outspoken about the of the world, while Laura was the milquetoast, All-Lives-Matter activist.

Thomas simply looked outside at the never-ending farms that were filled with a prosperity that would only last if an uncaring god willed it. They seemed to encompass all of Virginia, as though they had yet to arrive at the airport.

Trump can only make America great again if he can make my household great again—which he has not.

"If it weren't for the damn Chinese…" Dominic muttered.

"Don't say that in front of your son," his mother warned.

Thomas knew that his mother didn't accept the derogatory remarks. For one, she didn't believe in judging an entire group of people because it involved shifting the blame onto other people. He noticed that she never blamed the electrical company for laying off Dominic.

Perhaps that is why she is so successful.

Of course, the reason for it was because Laura went to college in California and was self-conscious of the stereotypes of the Virginia hick, so she taught herself to speak Standard American English and avoided any of the accent inflections. Years later, she still has that standardized accent and the work ethic that followed.

Of course, I don't know if that work ethic would mean anything when the chips are down, and a pandemic goes around.

After Dominic walked outside, he seated himself inside the car, waiting for Laura. As soon as she walked outside, she gestured Thomas to come over so she could hug him. After embracing, she told Thomas, "Take care of your sister."

"I will."

Dominic drove out of the parking space and toward the airport, where he entered an empty highway with vehicles far behind. Thomas didn't bring his iPhone to distract himself nor his homework to study complex equations.

I'm stuck with this asshole.

He couldn't think of anything to do other than observe the miles upon miles of farmland and empty acres, as though he was in a surreal sci-fi film where there is no tenable escape and that it's within a hellish simulacrum of boredom.

Dominic simply drove off in silence while Thomas felt consternation inside.

As Thomas and Ashley sat upon the porch in the entrance of their house, trying to take in the warm Virginia air that brushed through the countryside at this season. They already had central air conditioning in the house, yet the outdoors felt natural, as though a warm welcome back home after a long day of school.

Yet, the weather didn't feel smooth to Thomas somehow.

It feels as though we are the only ones who live in the Williams house with the vengeful spirits of every Williams ancestor haunting us—with Dominic somehow, yet I cannot put a word on it. I'm not threatened by him, yet somehow there is something fishy about him.

Thomas was suspicious about Dominic the moment they returned home. The only person he could tell it to would be his own sister.

So, he asked her, "Have you felt strange being with Ashley?" He was able to recognize whenever a friend's father was angry or depressed, and there was always some reason behind it

"I," she started. "I only want to give Dominic a chance. He lost his job, and I want you to do so also. The only strangeness I feel is when I think he might…"

Thomas noted Ashley's hesitation, as though she was about to pick herself and run off; however, she still sat on the porch, feeling its rickety wood. Yet, she never explained what she thought Dominic might be capable of doing.

She said, "It's probably paranoia."

"C'mon. You know I'm not paranoid."

Ashley chuckled.

They saw a car drive into the parking lot, with a girl that looked older than Ashley looking stressed about something Thomas couldn't understand. He and Ashley didn't bother to ask what she was doing or where she was going.

Perhaps she is lost? Yet maybe she has something to say.

When she got out of the car, she rushed over to the siblings and asked, "Are you Laura Williams' kids?"

They both responded that they were. The girl had brown curly hair that fell upon her shoulders.

Somehow, she would provide the answers I seek.

"My name is Jessie Turner, and I want to tell you that Dominic is not who he says he is."

"Well, he has not fooled me," Thomas told her. "I already know him to be an angry prick."

"It's more than just that," she exhaled, and she looked as though on the verge of crying. "He is capable of far more insidious things."

Ashley told her, "He's still at the airport, so maybe you can come inside to talk."

When they walked inside, they sat in the kitchen table with Kayla constantly looking at the window, expecting Dominic to come home.

She turned to Thomas and Ashley and told them, "You were never told why exactly my parents divorced. Dominic was abusive, constantly hitting me and Shannon, my mother. He told me mother than if he goes to prison for beating her, he will just come out worse and then come for us. So, my mother never filed any charges, and instead for a divorce."

Although it made sense to Thomas, Ashley looked surprised at how capable Dominic would be to engage in abusive behavior. Never had any of them been hit by him, for the only reason why Laura chose him was because of his hard work which matched her own.

I didn't marry you so you could screw us over. That was what she said to him. Would she really value hard work over safety?

Jessie continued, "I wish I could take you both with me. Where is Laura?"

"She is going on a business trip, which she insisted on going to."

"In the middle of a pandemic? That woman is crazy."

Thomas nearly snickered at that comment, which was one that he would have had when he first heard of her insistence.

She would make a great girlfriend.

"That's not the point. If she cannot be here to protect you, then I insist that you come with me."

"We haven't seen Dominic be abusive," Ashley said. "I'm sure that he has changed."

"You know," Jessie said as she twirled Ashley's blonde locks. "You reach an age when you start understanding that people you are close with are not infallible. I don't want you to take any chances."

Chapter 3

The ground felt hard against Thomas's knees as he tried to block Ashley's soccer ball from heading toward the goal. Although Thomas didn't need to do much, this time he felt numb to anything around him, since he barely got any sleep. The whole time he kept thinking about whether Dominic would start abusing them too, especially with Laura on a trip. Ashley, along with Travis, were more concerned with kicking the ball between her feet as she guided it toward the goalie, then she kicked it, and it whooshed past him.

"You're not even trying, Thomas," she told him. "Travis pays more attention than you."

"I've been thinking about what Jessie had been telling us. Do you really think that Dominic is going to start hitting us, too?"

"I wouldn't think so."

Then Thomas noticed that Dominic had been watching them out from the window, not as a casual glance or even rooting for them to practice, but as though he was about to catch them doing something wrong.

So, Thomas and Ashley stopped what they were doing and waited for Dominic to say something.

Which he did, by simply saying "You're doing good."

After he walked from the window, Thomas and Ashley looked toward each other, worried. Thomas said, "Is he suspicious of us?"

"Probably. Maybe he needs work done around the house."

"He would have told us if that was the case."

Then, Dominic called out to Thomas, "I need you to help me with the basement!"

Speak of the devil.

There were boxes upon boxes that needed to be rearranged, since they could end up being awash from any floods that would percolate through the house's exterior. Thomas could see that inside were spare car parts in case the car broke down, as well as old magazines from twenty years ago. However, the most important attention was given to the recently purchased items from months ago, such as the lamps and the paint.

"They are really inflammable, so don't place them near the outlets."

Thomas waddled with one of the boxes in his arms as he guided it toward the heap of old boxes. He gently placed it atop one of the lower level boxes and snugged it in place.

Dominic carried one of boxes and asked, "How long have you worked in electrical engineering?"

"A long time. Ever since I graduated high school."

Since Thomas couldn't get a more detailed answer from Dominic, he decided to let the basement be filled with silence. He simply continued to place the boxes in the right place.

Then Dominic said, "Just follow your dreams. I don't know what I should say."

You could just say you want to leave this family in peace like you left your previous family.

As soon as Thomas was done with one section of the boxes, he asked Dominic, "Do you need any more work done?"

"No, you can go. Just remember that I will always be your new father."

Then, Thomas walked up the wooden stairs, keeping a steady pace to not sound like he was running upwards. Upon looking outside, he could see that Ashley and Travis were taking a break by sitting upon the porch, taking in the warm air. She drank from her water canteen while Travis lapped up his water bowl.

I'm still not used to Dominic.

Instead of meeting with Ashley, he returned to his room, walking past the hallway that felt empty without Laura there.

Upon hearing Van Halen's Panama ringtone in his iPhone, he took it out of his pocket, fiddled with the screen, and answered his mother.

"How are you doing?" she asked him.

I cannot tell her yet about the abuse in Dominic's previous life. It would just get messy.

"We're fine."

"Are you helping around the house?"

"Yes."

"You're not talkative. Is everything *truly* alright?"

"I'm just worried about my future as an accountant."

"I'm sure that we will all help you."

After updating her about the basement getting cleaned and Ashley continuing her practice, Thomas was told by Laura that he could rest for the day, especially since he had an entire weekend to study for the algebra test.

After hanging up the phone, he put it in the drawer of his nightstand and threw himself upon the bed.

***

Dinner was uncomfortable for Thomas, since no one spoke as they sat around the table. Although the chicken was well-done, every taste that Thomas took didn't satisfy him because he felt that any joy in the dinner wouldn't last long. Thomas could see that Dominic held his knife firmly which cautioned him a little. Instead of looking like cutting into meat, Dominic cut as though it was through bone. Ashley kept her head down on the mashed potatoes and broccoli. The meal was simple yet satisfying enough to Thomas, which he could only finish a single dish.

"Did your mother call you?" Dominic asked Thomas.

"Yes," Thomas told him. "I assured her that everything was fine."

"Good."

***

Yet another night was spent lying upon his bed, still wondering whether Jessie was right to think that Dominic could return to his abusive ways. While the rest of the world was in silence, there was a mental maelstrom inside Thomas. His heart kept beating fast and his started feeling a cold sweat upon his face.

Thomas heard Ashley's shriek.

He jumped out of bed and looked toward the door, intent on breaking it down and rushing toward his sister's room. The walls turned black and red, and he smelled rancid smoke coming from them.

I have to get Ashley out.

After slamming the door open, he ran toward her room as he could see there were flames everywhere.

From behind, Dominic wrapped his arm around Thomas's neck and put him into a chokehold, attempting to suffocate him. He threw himself backward to keep Thomas from resisting. Indeed, Thomas tried to back-kick Dominic to break free. However,

he was powerless to stop him.

Dominic snarled, "You're not the man

of the house, nor ever will be."

"Screw you, old man."

"You have no idea how much a job

loss can really cut off a man's manhood."

Thomas noticed that Ashley's door

was wide open, as though she ran off to call

the police. He never noticed Ashley run out

of the room.

All around him the fires spread

throughout the interior of the house,

appearing through the walls and the

windows. Thomas could feel the heat become more pertinent on his skin, as though the flames would consume him and Dominic.

I don't want to die in this house.

Just as the house and Dominic's arm turned black, there were loud, police sirens in the distance. Before slowly losing consciousness, he heard orders and shouts; and felt the police pull Dominic off of him.

Two police officers picked Thomas up and dragged him out of the burning house, while Thomas kept feeling the lick of flames that were increasing all around him.

Smoke filled his nostrils as though the

whole interior of the house was burning. By

the time Thomas was brought outside next

to Ashley, he had passed out.

***

When he awakened, Thomas saw that the

house had been nearly burnt to its

foundation, with the basement turned to

black and the holes that percolated

throughout the walls of the first and second

floors. But the most striking detail was that

the ivy bush was completely burnt off, as

though it was the first to catch fire.

Next to him, Jessie, who drove Thomas back to the house, told him, "When he left, I cried throughout the night. I had a mixture of emotions. I was glad that he no longer abused us, but also sad that I may never love a man again."

"You should not be hard on yourself."

"What *you* should have done was listened to me and left. Thankfully, Ashley called the police just in time."

Then she embraced him.

"I'm just glad that you're both safe."

"We still need to testify against him, and I'm quite nervous."

"We will be with you."

Thomas guided Jessie to the exterior of the house and pointed to the charcoaled spot where the ivy bush used to be.

He told her, "The house was distinguished by an ivy bush that had grown there for generations. It had a sort of ancient value to the house, as though it was a relic from the colonial days."

"So, has it lost its value, then? Of course, besides the fact that…" She didn't want to say that it was because the house was burnt down that it lost value, though Thomas understood when he responded,

"My mom informed me that she would have the house completely renovated as soon as she got home. She doesn't necessarily like living in the past."